NORMAN
PRICE

BELLA
LASAGNE

JAMES

SARAH

TITLES AVAILABLE IN BUZZ BOOKS

THOMAS THE TANK ENGINE

1   Thomas in trouble
2   Toby and the Stout Gentleman
3   Percy runs away
4   Thomas and the Breakdown Train
5   Edward, Gordon and Henry
6   Thomas goes Fishing
7   Thomas down the Mine
8   James and the Troublesome Trucks
9   Gordon off the Rails
10   Thomas and Terence
11   James and the Tar Wagons
12   Thomas and Bertie
13   Thomas and the Trucks
14   Thomas's Christmas Party

FIREMAN SAM

1   Trevor's Trial Run
2   Norman's Spooky Night
3   A Bad Day for Dilys
4   Bella and the Bird's Nest
5   The Pride of Pontypandy
6   A Surprise for Sarah
7   Elvis's Experiment
8   Christmas in Pontypandy

TUGS

1   Kidnapped
2   Run Aground
3   Nothing to Declare
4   Treasure Hunt

BUGS BUNNY

1   Ali Baba Bunny
2   Knighty Knight Bugs
3   Broomstick Bunny
4   Mutiny on the Bunny

BARNEY

1   Barney and the Picnic
2   Barney's New Hair-Do
3   Barney Goes Shopping
4   Barney's Happy Christmas

MICRO MACHINES

1   Road Block
2   Hijack
3   Safe Breakers
4   Snowbound

GREMLINS

1   Don't Get Wet
2   Midnight Feast

First published 1990 by Buzz Books,
an imprint of the Octopus Publishing Group,
Michelin House, 81 Fulham Road, London, SW3 6RB.

LONDON MELBOURNE AUCKLAND

Fireman Sam © 1985 Prism Art & Design Ltd.

Text © 1990 William Heinemann Ltd.

Illustrations © 1990 William Heinemann Ltd.
Story by Caroline Hill-Trevor
Illustrations by CLIC!
Based on the animation series produced by Bumper Films for
S4C/Channel 4 Wales and Prism Art & Design Ltd.
Original idea by Dave Gingell and Dave Jones, assisted by
Mike Young. Characters created by Rob Lee.
All rights reserved.

ISBN 1 85591 030 6

Printed and bound in the UK by BPCC Paulton Books Ltd.

THE PRIDE OF PONTYPANDY

Story by Caroline Hill-Trevor
Illustrations by CLIC!

Sarah and James were shopping with Bella,
choosing a present for Norman. "The
invisible ink or this?" asked Sarah, holding
up a black hairy spider.

"Ooh, I don't know," grinned James.

"Norman would like both of those. Let's get him the ink *and* the spider!"

"Hurry up now, you two, if we no go, we miss the bus," said Bella, anxiously looking at her watch.

"About time too," grumbled Trevor when
they got back to the bus. "Half an hour late.
You're lucky we didn't go without you."

"We're sorry, Trevor," said Sarah, "we
couldn't decide . . ."

8

"Come on, jump in quick now. Let's get going before this fog gets any worse."

When everyone was in, Trevor started the bus and set off towards Pontypandy.

As they drove along the fog got thicker.

9

"Real pea soup, this is," muttered Trevor, peering through the windscreen. "Good thing I know the road, it is." He slowed down to take the corner.

"Oooh, hold on tight everyone," he gasped, slamming on the brakes.

The bus stopped just in time. "Seems to be
something across the road," said Trevor,
jumping out to have a look. "Bloomin'
'eck!" he shouted, "there's been a landslide.
The road's completely blocked – we'll have
to go round the other way."

But as he climbed back into the bus there
was a big rumble and earth started rolling
down the bank until the road behind the
bus was covered.

"Oh my goodness," Trevor cried.
"Now we can't go backwards or forwards.
We're trapped! I wish Fireman Sam was
here. He'd know what to do."

"Shouldn't we call the fire brigade?" shouted James from the back of the bus.

"I'll nip back down the road to the call box," said Trevor. "But first, everyone must get out of the bus. You'll be much safer further up the road, and you can stop any more cars from coming down here."

At Pontypandy Fire Station, Firefighter
Penny Morris was putting Fireman Sam,
Fireman Elvis Cridlington and even
Station Officer Steele through their paces.

"Two and two, three and two, four and
two; that's it Fireman Sam," she chanted.
"You need to be strong to be a firefighter."

14

Penny turned to Station Officer Steele.
"Come on, Sir, stretch those legs!"

"Oh look," said Station Officer Steele,
jumping up. "There's a message coming
through on the printer. I'm sorry, everyone,
but it looks as if we'll have to finish our
exercises for today."

"Pontypandy to Newtown road blocked by landslide," read Fireman Sam, "bus and passengers trapped."

"Sounds like a job for the rescue tender," said Elvis, beaming at Penny.

"Yes, but landslides can be very

dangerous. We'll need all the strength
we've got — you'd better bring Jupiter, too."

"You go with Penny, Fireman Sam,"
ordered Station Officer Steele. "Elvis and I
will follow you in Jupiter." With the sirens
blaring, the convoy set off.

17

A few minutes later, they arrived at the scene. Sarah, James, Bella and Dilys were shivering by the side of the road.

"You did very well to get all your passengers out, Auxiliary Fireman Evans. Good show," said Station Officer Steele.

18

"What about my bus?" wailed Trevor.

"Right," said Station Officer Steele,
"standard landslide procedure."

"Yes, but what's that, Sir?" asked Elvis.

"Well then, um, let's see now . . ."
stuttered Station Officer Steele.

"Dig," said Fireman Sam. "Let's get out the spades and dig tracks in the earth so we can tow the bus out."

"Here you are, Elvis, borrow one of mine," said Penny, handing him a spade from the back of the rescue tender.

"Ooo, thanks, Penny," said Elvis, trying not to blush.

"Come on now, one two, one two, put your backs into it," said Penny, as she shovelled the soil out of the way. "This is hard work. Didn't I say you need to be strong to be a firefighter?"

"I thought we'd finished our exercises for today," muttered Station Officer Steele, wiping his brow.

"Hurry up," shouted Fireman Sam.
"There's more earth coming down. We
haven't got much time." They all put their
heads down and dug as fast as they could.

Before long, they had made tracks
through the earth.

"Right then," said Fireman Sam. "Now all we need to do is attach a towrope and pull the bus out. Trevor, you get in so you can steer. And don't look so worried, a good wash and your bus will be good as new again."

"We'll clean it for you," called James and Sarah together.

Trevor climbed into the bus but jumped out again immediately.

"Now what's wrong, Trevor?" said Station Officer Steele impatiently.

"There's a t.t.t.tarantula in my seat, Sir," stuttered Trevor.

"Impossible, Evans," bellowed Station Officer Steele.

"You must be seeing things. Fireman Sam, you have a look."

"Oh no!" James whispered to Sarah, "we're really in trouble now. You must have dropped Norman's present when you got out of the bus."

"Looks like Norman's been here!" said
Fireman Sam, winking at Sarah and James
as he held up the toy spider. "You'd better
keep this behind bars, Sarah, or you won't
be travelling by bus again!"

"Come on now," said Penny, "my tender's not strong enough for towing. We'd better use Jupiter. Please will you take the wheel, Fireman Sam?" Fireman Sam climbed into the cab and started the engine.

27

Towed by Jupiter, the bus slid out of the mud easily and was soon back on firm ground again. "There you are, Trevor," said Station Officer Steele.

"Thank you very much for your help, Firefighter Morris," said Fireman Sam.

"It was nothing," said Penny, looking at the group of beaming firemen. "Without Jupiter and you four firemen no one would even be able to see Trevor's bus by now. They don't call you The Pride of Pontypandy for nothing!"

FIREMAN SAM

STATION OFFICER STEELE

TREVOR EVANS

ELVIS CRIDLINGTON

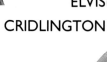

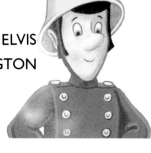

PENNY MORRIS